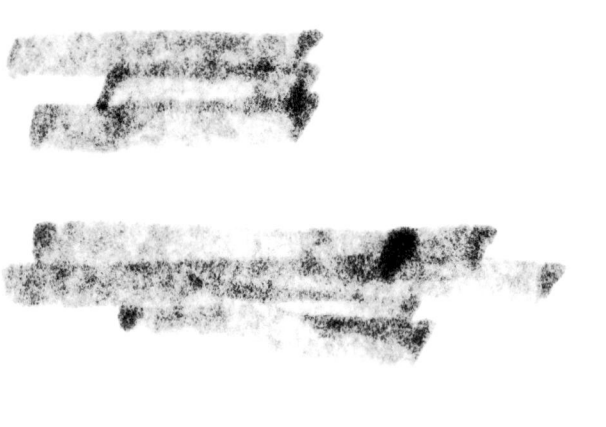

Tracing Our ENGLISH Roots

SHARON MOSCINSKI

John Muir Publications
Santa Fe, New Mexico

Special thanks to David M. De Polo, Santa Fe, New Mexico

John Muir Publications, P.O. Box 613, Santa Fe, New Mexico 87504
© 1995 by John Muir Publications
All rights reserved. Published 1995.
Printed in the United States of America

First edition. First printing January 1995
　　　　　　First TWG printing January 1995

Library of Congress Cataloging-in-Publication Data
Moscinski, Sharon.
American origins: tracing our English roots / Sharon Moscinski. - 1st ed.
　p.　　cm.
　Includes index.
　ISBN 1-56261-188-7 : $12.95
1. British Americans—History—Juvenile literature. 2. United States—History—Colonial period, ca. 1600-1775—Juvenile literature. 3. Great Britain—History—Medieval period, ca. 1066-1485—Juvenile literature. 4. Great Britain—History—Tudors, 1485-1603. I. Title.
E184.B7M67 1995
973'.0421—dc20　　　　　　　　　　　　　　94-26925
　　　　　　　　　　　　　　　　　　　　　　CIP

Production: Kathryn Lloyd-Strongin, Chris Brigman
Editorial: Elizabeth Wolf, Jo Ann Baldinger
Logo design: Peter Aschwanden
Interior design: Ken Wilson
Illustrations: Tony D'Agostino
Typesetting: Marcie Pottern
Printer: Quebecor Printing/Kingsport

Distributed to the book trade by
W. W. Norton & Co., Inc.
500 Fifth Avenue
New York, New York 10110

Distributed to the education market by
Wright Group Publishing, Inc.
19201 120th Avenue N.E.
Bothell, WA 98011-9512

Cover photo: Young cotton mill workers, ca. 1890, The Bettmann Archive
Title page photo: Young worker at a Massachusetts textile mill, The Bettmann Archive
Contents page photo: The *Mayflower*, Library of Congress
Back cover photo: The English Kitchen, Round Pond, Oklahoma, ca. 1890,
　National Archives and Records Administration

CONTENTS

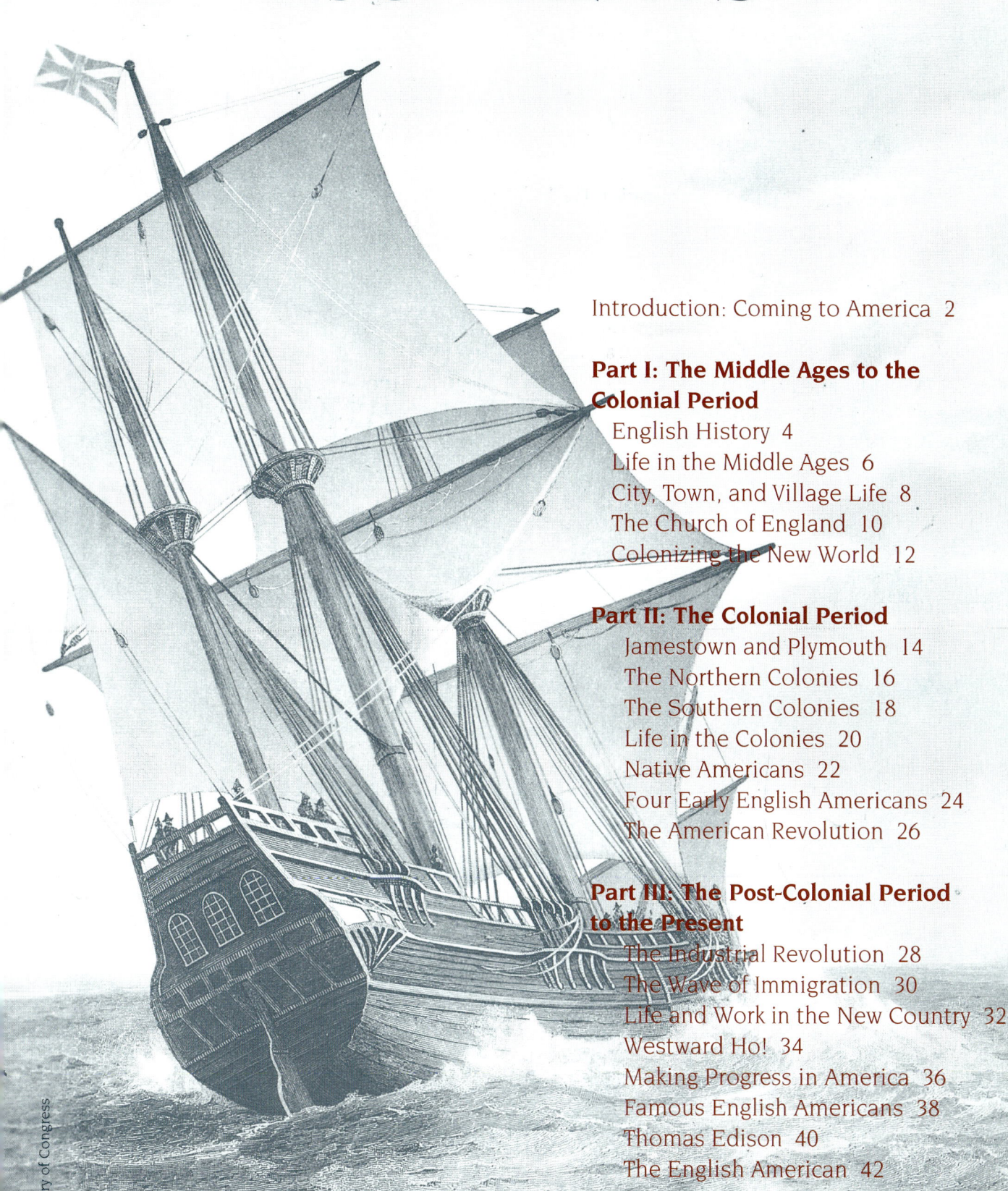

Introduction: Coming to America 2

Part I: The Middle Ages to the Colonial Period
English History 4
Life in the Middle Ages 6
City, Town, and Village Life 8
The Church of England 10
Colonizing the New World 12

Part II: The Colonial Period
Jamestown and Plymouth 14
The Northern Colonies 16
The Southern Colonies 18
Life in the Colonies 20
Native Americans 22
Four Early English Americans 24
The American Revolution 26

Part III: The Post-Colonial Period to the Present
The Industrial Revolution 28
The Wave of Immigration 30
Life and Work in the New Country 32
Westward Ho! 34
Making Progress in America 36
Famous English Americans 38
Thomas Edison 40
The English American 42

Index 45

COMING TO AMERICA

The first English colonists came to America in the early 1600s. They were English citizens who left their homeland to create new settlements, called colonies, in such places as Jamestown, Virginia and Plymouth, Massachusetts. These colonies then became part of the British Empire.

In the New World, English colonists lived very much as they had back at home. They spoke the English language, practiced English customs, and remained loyal to the king and queen of England. In many ways, the colonies were like "mini-Englands" across the Atlantic Ocean.

In 1690, almost 90 percent of all Europeans living in North America were English. The rest were mainly German, French, Spanish, Scottish, Irish, or Scandinavian. Because these other ethnic groups were so outnumbered by the English, they too began adopting English ways.

Many English colonists came to America to find religious freedom. Back in England, the Church of England was the only legal religion. Some people, called dissenters, wanted to belong to different religious groups, but they were not permit-

English immigrants quickly found jobs in America

How Many English Came to America?

Decade	Number
1607-1785	2,500,000
1820-1830	26,336
1831-1840	74,350
1841-1850	208,572
1851-1860	445,324
1861-1870	606,896
1871-1880	578,046
1881-1890	807,357
1891-1900	282,438
1901-1910	525,953
1911-1920	341,308
1921-1930	330,163
1931-1940	29,378
1941-1950	141,592
1951-1960	191,514

The English began coming to America in the 1600s, but real records were not kept until 1820. These numbers include all immigrants from Great Britain, which is made up of England, Scotland, and Wales.

English colonists set sail for the New World in 1607

ted to do so. They were fined, thrown in jail, or even killed. As a result, some dissenters decided to build colonies in America where they could worship as they pleased.

Most of the colonists, however, came to America to improve their lot in life. By the middle to late 1600s, the colonies had become very prosperous. Thousands of English men and women decided to take advantage of the opportunities available in the New World.

In the northern colonies, English immigrants became carpenters, craftsmen, dockhands, or merchants. In the South, they worked on large plantations tilling the soil, sowing seeds, and harvesting crops. Others ventured out to the western plains and became pioneer farmers.

By the time of the Revolutionary War (1775–1783), when the colonists won their independence from England, many English colonists had been in America for generations. The war was fought largely because England demanded that the colonists pay unfair taxes. Another reason was that many colonists no longer felt loyal to England. It is interesting to realize that *before* the Revolutionary War the colonists were English men and women living in America. *After* the Revolutionary War they were English Americans.

In the 1800s, some 3 million English people came to America. Unlike their colonial ancestors, they were not just settling in an English colony, but were moving to an entirely different country. All the same, the English had quite a bit in common with Americans. As a result, they found work quickly and became successful faster than any other immigrant group.

Tracing Our English Roots tells the story of the millions of English men and women who came to America from the 1600s to the present. The story of these English immigrants is a very significant one. They formed and shaped this country more than any other ethnic group because, to a great extent, they founded it. As you read this book, remember that you are not just reading about English Americans. You are also reading about the creation of the United States of America.

PART I: THE MIDDLE AGES TO THE COLONIAL PERIOD

ENGLISH HISTORY

One thousand years ago, England was a weak island nation. Small villages were scattered throughout the lush, green countryside. Tribal peoples such as the Celts, Vikings, Normans, Angles, and Saxons lived in these villages. But things changed in A.D. 1066. In that year, William the Conqueror, leader of the Normans, defeated Harold II, king of the Saxons, and claimed the English throne for himself.

As king, William oversaw a system called feudalism. Under this system, the king owned all the land in England. He gave some of the land to the Catholic Church, which was very powerful, and the rest to his lords. In return, the lords pledged their loyalty to the king. They gave their advice in matters of government and helped defend England from invaders.

Each lord ruled his parcel of land, called a manor. The lord kept some land for himself and divided the rest among the peasants, called villeins (VILL-ens) and serfs. Villeins received a few acres of land for which they had to pay rent, usually in the form of labor and gifts. Serfs were practically slaves. They worked for food and shelter.

The king was expected to ask the Great Council—a group of lords and barons—for its opinion before making any decisions about things like taxes and wars. Many English rulers, such as King John, ignored

English philosopher John Locke

John Locke (1632–1714) was a famous English philosopher who thought a lot about politics and government. Locke believed that every person had political power. Governments were formed when groups of individuals gave their consent—or agreed—to let other people rule them. Locke stated that all human beings were born equal, and that it was a natural right to pursue "life, health, liberty, and possessions." He also defended the freedom of thought and speech. Locke's ideas paved the way for American democracy by influencing the Founding Fathers, especially Thomas Jefferson.

the Great Council. This made the English nobles very angry. So in 1215 they forced King John to sign the Magna Carta, which in Latin means the "Great Charter."

The Magna Carta limited the power of the king in very important ways. For example, he no longer could punish people he did not like. Instead, citizens were guaranteed trial by jury. Although at first the Magna Carta only protected the upper classes, gradually more rights were granted to other people as well.

In addition, the king had to listen to the Great Council in matters of government. He could not raise taxes as he pleased, and he was required to obey the law just like everyone else. Otherwise, the Great Council could declare war on the king and take away his right to rule.

Nevertheless, Parliament (which replaced the Great Council in the mid-1200s) and English kings continued to struggle for power. The situation became worse during the reign of Charles I. For 11 years—from 1629 to 1640—Charles did not ask Parliament for its advice at all. He engaged England in costly wars, raised taxes enormously, and made many enemies.

In 1215, King John signed the Magna Carta, which paved the way for democracy

As a result, in 1642 a clever military man named Oliver Cromwell led a civil war against King Charles and his supporters. Cromwell won the war, and King Charles was beheaded. His death taught future rulers of England that it could be dangerous to ignore Parliament. Parliament then passed the Bill of Rights. It promised English citizens many of the same rights later included in the American Bill of Rights, such as freedom of speech.

Peasants worked for wealthy noblemen during the Middle Ages

LIFE IN THE MIDDLE AGES

The period of European history known as the Middle Ages, or medieval times, lasted from about A.D. 1100 to 1500. To medieval peasants, the world was small. Many never set foot outside their village their entire lives. They worked hard on their land from sunrise to sunset. And they had little chance to improve their lives.

Most medieval villages contained three fields of land. Each year, two of these fields grew crops and the third was left fallow—meaning it was left unplanted to improve the quality of the soil. At harvest time, the peasants had to give one-tenth (a tithe) of their crop to the parish church and another portion to the lord as payment of rent. Whatever was left over they could keep for themselves.

The peasants ate simple meals of bread and ale, a type of beer, rounded out with vegetables, milk, and cheese. On special occasions they enjoyed meat dishes. A typical family lived in a small cottage built from wood and mud. The cottage was surrounded by a plot of land, called a croft, where the family grew vegetables and kept hens, pigs, and other livestock.

When darkness fell, the cottages were dimly lit by a rushlight—a candle made from the stem of a rush plant dipped in fat. The peasants slept on mattresses stuffed with straw and kept warm under coarse, homemade blankets. Life was hard, rough, and often short—death from starvation or disease always lurked just around the corner. People were haunted by fears of demons and devils; they believed in ghosts, spirits, and the "evil eye."

Medieval peasants often took religious trips called pilgrimages

The Bettmann Archive

Feast days and festivals provided a welcome break for the hardworking peasants. During these festivities, they enjoyed roasts, ale, and special foods. Children were entertained by jugglers, jesters, and storytellers, and merrily sang and danced to popular tunes. Others gambled on contests in shooting, wrestling, running, and hurling iron bars. Plays, games, fairs, and drinking contests at local taverns also softened the struggles of day-to-day life.

Religion was very important to the peasants. On Sundays, the villagers gathered at the local church to attend Mass. The church also hosted such festive events as weddings, christenings, and celebrations of religious holidays. The parish priest was usually the only person in the village who could read and write. He taught the peasants passages from the Bible, helped them in times of need, and lectured them about morality.

The medieval peasants were uneducated and poor, and had few opportunities. Their way of life remained more or less the same for over 400 years. Strangely, it was a horrible disaster that gave them a chance to improve their lives at last.

In 1348 and 1349, Europe and Asia were struck by the bubonic plague. Between one-third and one-half of the European population died. Every English village was hit by the Black Death, as it came to be called. Often whole families died, and their farms were left deserted. The surviving peasants claimed these farms as their own. They hired farmhands to help with the work and made big profits.

This situation created a class of independent farmers, people who worked for themselves rather than for a wealthy lord. These farmers had the money and leisure to educate themselves, and they demanded more rights. Free peasants moved to towns, which began to grow in number and size throughout England. The townspeople started to organize local governments, trade goods and services, and hold weekly markets. Lords became less and less powerful, and by the early 1500s, the dark age of feudalism finally came to an end.

In the mid-1300s, a terrible plague killed half the population of England

Rich and poor alike celebrated during festivals and feast days

CITY, TOWN, AND VILLAGE LIFE

In the 1500s, English villages grew into towns and towns blossomed into cities. By the late 1600s, towns such as York and Bristol each boasted a population of over 30,000. London, which was a worldwide center of trade, housed as many as 200,000 people.

Port cities such as Liverpool became wealthy by bringing in cotton and tobacco from the American colonies. Other cities were famous for their silk businesses, shipbuilding yards, or iron and steel industries. There were many different ways to make money. Finally, families could support themselves in jobs other than farming.

The large towns and cities hustled and bustled with activity. Merchants, craftsmen, servants, and street vendors all hurried past each other in the narrow streets. Horse-drawn carriages rolled from one end of town to the other, carrying people or goods.

Cities, especially London, had hundreds of taverns, pubs, and inns that stayed open all day and all night. Tea, coffee, and hot chocolate were brand new, trendy drinks. Betting on the results of cock-fighting games was a popular—if brutal—pastime. But there were also more peaceful forms of entertainment, like puppet shows, plays, jugglers, and huge fairs.

Town and city life could be quite exciting, but the living conditions of the average person were still poor. Houses were huddled close together on narrow roads that received little sunlight. Trash lay on the streets to rot, and city lanes became smelly breeding grounds for disease.

However, many English people in the late 1600s and early 1700s were still farmers living in rural villages. During this time, new farm tools were being designed. For example, Jethro Tull invented the seed drill, which

William Shakespeare, playwright and poet

Plays were popular pastimes for rich and poor alike. The wealthier citizens sat in comfortable seats while the poorer, often rowdy theatergoers stood in front of the stage. William Shakespeare (1564–1616) was one of England's most popular playwrights. His greatness came from his poetic and masterful use of the English language. Today, Shakespeare's plays are performed more often and in more countries than those of any other writer in history.

By the late 1500s, London was a center for world trade

planted seeds quickly into the soil at the right depth. He also designed the horse hoe, which made weeding easier.

Because of these and other new tools, more food could be grown on less land. As a result, there was enough food to feed the growing population, and farmers earned more money.

Farmers found they made even more money by farming one large area of land rather than many small plots in the open fields. They could do this by buying land from their neighbors. When neighbors did not want to sell, however, they were often cheated or forced to sell their land at unfair prices.

Each village usually had a meadow and pasture that belonged to all of the villagers. They grazed animals, collected firewood, and hunted wild game on this land. But beginning in the late 1500s, greedy landowners began claiming these areas for themselves. The villagers did not have the money or the know-how to get back their land. Without it, small farmers could not manage, and many lived on the brink of starvation.

When these families lost their land, they became poorly paid, overworked farm laborers, or moved into towns hoping to find jobs. Although some people prospered on large farms or in cities and towns, the majority had become very poor and had to depend on charity.

City streets bustled with activity in the 1600s

THE CHURCH OF ENGLAND

During the Middle Ages most Europeans, including the English, belonged to the Roman Catholic Church. The Catholic Church was ruled by the pope in Rome, Italy. It owned monasteries, estates, and great stretches of land throughout Europe. It was very rich and very powerful.

English kings and queens, like most European rulers, claimed that their right to rule was given by God. So they were careful to stay on good terms with the pope. Otherwise, they risked being excommunicated, or thrown out of the Church. When the pope excommunicated kings or queens, he took away their right to rule.

English monarchs struggled against the power of the pope for centuries. This struggle finally exploded during the reign of Henry VIII (1509–1547). Henry was married to Catherine of Aragon, but he wanted a divorce. He asked the pope for permission to divorce Catherine and marry Anne Boleyn. The pope denied Henry's request.

Henry got even by cutting all ties between England and the Catholic Church. With the support of Parliament, Henry began a new religious group in 1534 called the Church of England. This was to be a national church, headed by the king or queen of England.

Parliament supported the Church of England chiefly for political rather than religious reasons. King Henry was now in charge of government *and* religion. England

A Catholic named Guy Fawkes tried to blow up the Parliament building

Many English men and women remained Catholic, and they were often persecuted. A group of radical Catholics, led by Guy Fawkes, planned to blow up the Parliament building while King James and his chief advisors met inside. But the plot was discovered. Fawkes was arrested on Nov. 4, 1605 and hanged for his crime. In England, Guy Fawkes Day is still celebrated every November 5 by setting off fireworks and burning a make-believe image of "Guy" in a large bonfire.

King Henry VIII of England

could make more independent decisions because it no longer had to worry about angering the pope. Also, England became a much richer country because Henry took away the many properties owned by the Catholic Church and sold them to the highest bidder.

However, Henry needed the whole nation to support the Church of England. So he passed a law demanding that every man and woman must support the Church of England. Protestors were fined, jailed, or sentenced to death.

Henry also tried to make the new Church a source of national pride. For the first time, Mass was said in English, not Latin, the language of the clergy. Every parish church used the same Prayer Book and had a Bible translated into English. Priests were allowed to marry, and people who did not attend Mass were publicly scolded.

During the reign of Henry's daughter, Queen Elizabeth I (1558–1603), there were a number of people who complained that the Church of England was still too "Catholic." Members of this group were called Puritans because they wanted to purify the Church of England by doing away with the rituals and practices handed down from Catholicism. A more radical group, called Separatists, wanted to separate from the Church of England and begin yet another new religion.

The next ruler after Elizabeth, James I (1603–1625), had no patience with the Puritans. James told the Puritans that if they did not support the Church of England, he would torture them until they left England. Puritans were forbidden to hold political office, and they were fined, put in prison, or even burned alive. The Separatists received the cruelest punishments, and in 1609 some of them fled to Holland in search of religious freedom.

Canterbury Cathedral, the headquarters of the Church of England

COLONIZING THE NEW WORLD

Spain began establishing colonies in North America shortly after Christopher Columbus arrived in the New World in 1492. France started a colony in North America in 1534, which became very large. Both countries made great profits from these possessions.

For many years, England was not interested in starting colonies in the New World. This changed in 1588 when Spain sent a powerful fleet of ships, called the Spanish Armada, to attack England. England's navy completely destroyed the Armada, proving itself to be the mightiest navy in the world. After its victory, England

Spanish conquistadors explored the New World in the 1500s

wanted to show off its naval power and became eager to colonize the New World.

Adventurous businessmen were among the first supporters of colonization. The explorers Sir Humphrey Gilbert and his half-brother Sir Walter Raleigh tried several times

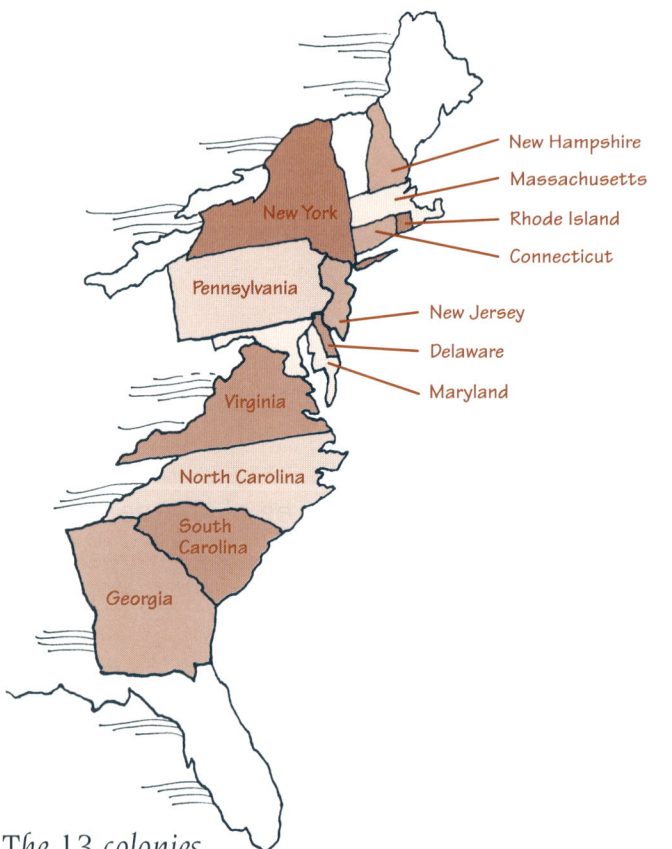

The 13 colonies

Between 1607 and 1775, the English government sent about 50,000 criminals to the colonies. Why? Because the prisons in England had become overcrowded. To solve this problem, criminals were often sentenced to forced labor in the colonies. Some returned to England when their terms were up. But the majority were won over by the opportunities in America and chose to stay.

The Pilgrims landed at Plymouth Rock in 1620

to found an English colony in the New World, but they failed. Finally, in 1607 the Jamestown colony in Virginia was established to make a profit for investors in London.

Puritans desperately needed to find a place where they could worship freely after King James I died in 1625. James had treated the Puritans harshly. But the new king, Charles I, tormented them even more.

Although it was dangerous for Puritans to remain in England, it was also dangerous to sail to the New World. The voyage lasted three months or longer. During the trip, passengers had to live in the dark hulls of overcrowded ships. They suffered from constant seasickness and were rarely given enough food and water. In addition, many fell ill from diseases that spread quickly in the cramped and dirty quarters. Even so, beginning in 1620 thousands of Puritans braved these risks to begin their lives anew in the New World.

Most Puritan immigrants were educated, middle-class merchants, traders, and craftsmen. Armed with their belief in thrift and hard work, they built prosperous and thriving homes in the New World.

After 1689, Puritans immigrated to the American colonies in much smaller numbers. In that year, William and Mary, the new king and queen of England, granted religious freedom to Puritans. Guaranteed the right to worship, Puritans had fewer reasons to leave their homeland.

However, at the same time unemployment was spreading like wildfire throughout England. Small farmers were being pushed off the land by greedy landowners. There were no other jobs for these farmers. Many families had to depend on charity.

The English government offered to ship unemployed workers, free of charge, to the colonies in America. Land was plentiful there, and people were needed to work on the large plantations in the South. In the long run, it was cheaper for the government to send the unemployed to America than it was to keep them on charity. This twist of fate let thousands of poor farmers make a fresh start in America.

PART II: THE COLONIAL PERIOD

JAMESTOWN AND PLYMOUTH

Jamestown was the first successful English colony in the New World. It was founded in May 1607 by 104 English adventurers who landed near the mouth of the James River in Virginia. These first settlers were all men. A few English women came to the colony after 1611, but women did not immigrate in large numbers until 1619.

Jamestown was settled mainly for business purposes. The Virginia Company in England provided ships and supplies for the journey to the New World. In return, the settlers were to send valuable goods found in the new land back to England.

The settlers expected to make quick money digging for gold or trading with the Indians for furs. To survive, however, they had to clear the land of trees, build houses, hunt for food, and plant and harvest crops. Only a few of the men were skilled workers. All the rest were noblemen who were not used to working. Their hands blistered easily, and they became sore and weak from the hard labor.

By mid-summer, the settlers had eaten all the food brought over from England. In addition, a nearby river, which provided the men with drinking water, grew shallow and slimy. The heat, foul water, hard work, and poor food allowed diseases like malaria

English settlers signed the Mayflower Compact before they landed at Plymouth Rock

Only about half of the *Mayflower* passengers were Pilgrims. The rest were faithful to the Church of England. They came to the colonies so they could own land. Because the colonists shared the food and tools brought over from England, it was important for them to stick together. But some threatened to leave the group and settle on their own. Before landing, the men on board signed the Mayflower Compact, an agreement to form one government and obey any laws that would be passed later.

The Jamestown colonists quickly began clearing land for homes and fields

and cholera to spread quickly throughout the colony. Almost three-quarters of the settlers died.

Tobacco saved the Jamestown colony. There was a huge demand for it in Europe. The colonist John Rolfe created a tobacco plant that suited European tastes. By growing tobacco, Virginia soon became a wealthy colony.

But Rolfe is perhaps best known for marrying Pocahontas, daughter of the Indian chief Powhatan. As a result of this marriage, relations between colonists and Indians remained peaceful. Powhatan's tribe gave the Jamestown colonists food and probably taught them how to grow corn and tobacco.

Plymouth, Massachusetts, was England's second colony. It was settled in December 1620 by a group of Puritan Separatists called Pilgrims. The Pilgrims came over on a ship called the *Mayflower*.

Plymouth had once been the home of an Indian tribe. It had a spring of pure drinking water, a hill for a fort and a lookout, and land already cleared for growing crops and corn.

Nevertheless, building shelters was hard work, and the Pilgrims were unused to the freezing New England winters. Also, they had not eaten fruits or vegetables for over four months. As a result, almost every member of the colony developed scurvy, a disease caused by a lack of vitamin C. Scurvy, cold, and constant labor made the Pilgrims defenseless against disease. By the end of their first winter, over half of the colonists had died.

The next spring, the Pilgrims met an Indian named Squanto. Squanto had gone to England with an explorer and spoke good English. He helped the Pilgrims thrive in their new and unfamiliar land.

Squanto taught them where to fish, how to cure illnesses using native herbs, what wild greens were good to eat, and most important, how to raise a good corn crop. That autumn's harvest was plentiful. To thank God for their good fortune, the Pilgrims planned a great feast. They invited some neighboring Indians, and together they celebrated America's first Thanksgiving.

Squanto taught the Pilgrims how to plant corn

THE NORTHERN COLONIES

After Plymouth and Jamestown, Massachusetts Bay became the third English colony in North America. It was founded in 1630 by a group of Puritans who wished to escape religious persecution in England. With an original population of about 1,000, Massachusetts Bay was the largest colony for many years. John Winthrop served 12 terms as governor of the colony, and Boston became its capital.

The Puritans came to Massachusetts Bay because they wanted to worship freely. But they were unwilling to grant religious freedom to others. Those who disagreed with the Puritans were banished, meaning they were forced to leave the community.

This was the fate of Reverend Roger Williams and Reverend Thomas Hooker. They were banished in 1635 because they found the Massachusetts Bay colony too

Shipbuilding was a major industry in the North

John Winthrop, governor of Massachusetts Bay

Witches are people said to have magical powers that can cause harm to others. Originally, they were probably people who healed illnesses using herbs and other natural methods. In the Middle Ages, many believed in witches and were afraid of them. In England, Spain, and other countries, thousands of innocent people, mostly women, were put to death by church officials. Fear of witches spread to the American colonies. In 1692, some famous witch trials were held in the village of Salem, Massachusetts. Many people were falsely accused of being witches, and 20 of them were hanged. Today, some people still practice Wiccan, an old religion that came to be called "witchcraft."

strict. Reverend Williams believed that government should not interfere with religion. He also said the colonists had no right to land unless they bought it from the Native Americans. In 1636 Williams helped establish the colony of Rhode Island, and Reverend Hooker and his followers colonized the Connecticut Valley.

The Society of Friends, often called Quakers, was also persecuted in England. William Penn, a respected Quaker, wanted to build a safe home for them in the New World. But the king or queen of England had to give permission before a new colony could be established.

The king at the time, Charles II, owed Penn quite a bit of money. Penn made a deal with the king: He would cancel the debt if the king allowed him to begin a colony. The king accepted, and in 1682 Penn and some fellow Quakers founded the colony of Pennsylvania.

The Quakers practiced religious tolerance. That meant they believed religious freedom should be a right for all Christians. As a result, people of many different religious groups were able to live peacefully together in Pennsylvania. Soon it had become the largest and most successful colony in the New World.

New York City was originally a Dutch colony named New Amsterdam. The English wanted it for themselves because it had a flourishing fur trade. In 1664, England set out to take over New Amsterdam. The Dutch colonists, who had no army or navy, surrendered without firing a shot. The area was then renamed New York after the Duke of York, the future King James II.

In most colonies, about 90 percent of the population was English. In New York, however, the population was more mixed. Dutch, Swedes, Swiss, and other Europeans had already settled in the area. In fact, by the late 1600s, 18 different languages were being spoken on Manhattan Island. New York was as much an ethnic mixture in its beginnings as it is today.

People suspected of practicing witchcraft were often put in stocks

THE SOUTHERN COLONIES

After Virginia, Maryland was the second colony to be established in the South. It was founded in 1634 by Cecil Calvert, a Roman Catholic. Along with Puritans, Catholics were persecuted in England, so Calvert made Maryland a safe place where Catholics could worship freely.

In 1663, King Charles II let eight noblemen settle Carolina, a colony south of Virginia. Carolina was later divided into North Carolina and South Carolina.

Georgia, the last English colony in the New World, was founded in 1732 by James Oglethorpe. It was settled by men who had been jailed in England for not paying their debts. The English hoped this colony would protect wealthy South Carolina from a possible attack from the Spanish in Florida.

The mild climate and rich soil of the South were ideal for farming. Growing tobacco had made Virginia quite wealthy, and the other southern colonies wanted to enjoy the same success. Large tobacco and rice plantations blossomed throughout Maryland, the Carolinas, and Georgia.

Around the mid-1700s, machines were invented to do jobs that used to be done by human beings. This period came to be called the Industrial Revolution. New machines in textile mills in England and the northern colonies could make huge quantities of cloth. But the mills first needed raw materials, especially cotton.

Harriet Beecher Stowe, author of Uncle Tom's Cabin

Many Amerians believed slavery was wrong and worked to abolish, or end, it. Harriet Beecher Stowe, an English American activist, wrote the famous anti-slavery novel *Uncle Tom's Cabin*. Stowe's book influenced the American people so greatly, it is considered one of the causes of the Civil War (1861–1865). During that war, President Abraham Lincoln freed the slaves with the Emancipation Proclamation.

To fill this great demand, many southern plantation owners found it more profitable to grow cotton on their land. But they needed many workers to grow, pick, clean, and ship cotton, or any other crop.

At first, most of this work was done by indentured servants. Indentured servants were usually English men and women who wanted to come to the colonies but could not afford the fares. People in the colonies would pay the servants' fares and give them food, clothing, and shelter. In return, the servants would work for the colonists for four to seven years. Afterwards, the servants were free to work for wages, buy land, and start a home.

There were not enough white indentured servants to fill the demand for workers. So plantation owners began buying and selling African slaves. Unlike white indentured servants, slaves could be forced to work their entire lives for no wages. They received no protection under English law and often were treated cruelly by the slave owners.

Men who bought and sold slaves became very wealthy, and the "slave trade" grew quickly. In 1690 there were only a few thousand slaves in the southern colonies.

In the South, the forced labor of African slaves was used to harvest crops

Wealthy southerners copied English styles and manners

But by 1790 there were more than 650,000. Usually the slaves were kidnapped by slave-traders from their homes in Africa, chained, and shoved into unbearably crowded ships. Once they reached the colonies, they were sold to the highest bidder at a slave auction. Often families were separated when fathers, mothers, or children were sold to different slave owners.

Slave owners defended slavery by claiming that Africans were less intelligent and less moral than whites and deserved to be enslaved. These racist attitudes, along with greed, kept slavery alive. The southern colonies became wealthy by using the forced labor of captive people. The northern colonies also got rich off of slavery because they paid little for the cotton and other crops grown cheaply in the South with slave labor. Also, many slave-traders were northern shippers.

19

LIFE IN THE COLONIES

Religion was the center of life in many colonies. Massachusetts was founded by Puritans, Pennsylvania by Quakers, and Maryland by Catholics. So we often think of the early colonists as people in search of religious freedom. Many were, but most colonists immigrated chiefly to improve their lot in life and find the American dream—even before there was an America!

In the North, the soil was not rich enough to support large plantations. Instead, the northern colonists worked to build their small communities into thriving centers of trade. They traded raccoon and fox pelts, exported lumber to England, and created giant shipbuilding and iron industries. The colonies soon produced one-seventh of the world's iron supply.

As the northern colonies became more advanced, new jobs and opportunities were created. Teachers, clergymen, lawyers, doctors, merchants, and skilled craftsmen were all in great demand. Trained professionals in the North enjoyed good wages, and new arrivals from England had little problem finding work.

Nevertheless, in the 1700s northern cities were few, and towns were small. In the center of a typical town was the meetinghouse. This building served as a gathering place for the community to worship, make decisions about the local government, or discuss important issues. Near the meetinghouse, blacksmiths, carpenters, cabinetmakers, and tailors had their shops.

The shops were surrounded by private houses and farms. At first houses were made out of wood and were finished with thatched roofs like those back in England. But such houses did not keep out the cold. Soon, warmer, sturdier homes were made from brick and topped with roofing tiles.

A spelling lesson at school

Excitement swept the country in 1789 when Noah Webster published his *American Spelling Book*, which became the authority on the correct spelling of words. Good spelling came to be seen as a sign of education and culture, and children spent many hours mastering this skill. At the urging of Benjamin Franklin, the now famous "spelling bee" became a wildly popular event in schools and rural communities throughout the country.

Families, especially among the Puritans, were often large. Children were taught to be useful and were given chores to do. Most colonists believed a good education would make a child successful in life, so each town tried to build a school. At the very least, children were taught to read so they could study the Bible. The schools in some prosperous cities, such as Philadelphia, Pennsylvania, offered classes in a wide range of subjects from navigation, to mathematics, to painting.

In the southern colonies, plantation owners tried to copy the lifestyle of the wealthy classes back in England. Many products were imported from England, even though similar items could be purchased locally for much less money. English leisure time activities like hunting and riding were popular. English manners and dress were seen as signs of a well-to-do upbringing.

Many southerners were freed indentured servants who became craftsmen, professionals, or more commonly, independent farmers. Land was plentiful, so farms were larger and houses were farther apart than in the North. It was often impossible to build a local school because most children lived too far away to attend. So they were taught either by their parents or by traveling teachers who gave lessons in private homes. In the 1700s, nearly one-half of children in the South could not read and write.

The village blacksmith was an important member of the community

Children helped with chores and often were educated at home

NATIVE AMERICANS

Tribal peoples lived throughout the New World for thousands of years before Europeans arrived. They came to be called Indians because Christopher Columbus thought he had landed in India in 1492. Indians, or Native Americans, were not one people but many independent groups. Each tribe had its own unique history and culture.

The Indians took pity on the first English colonists. They helped the colonists establish Rhode Island and Georgia, and they saved the Plymouth Pilgrims by giving them food and teaching them how to survive in the wilderness. However, many English settlers believed the Indians were inferior to them. They tried to enslave the Indians and convert them to Christianity, and they often stole their land.

Southern tobacco lords captured Indians to work on their plantations as slaves. The Indians resisted. They refused to work, ran away, or even killed themselves and their children rather than endure the bonds of slavery.

Just the same, the colonists and Indians often became trading partners. In Europe, furs were in fashion, and there was a great demand for fox and beaver pelts. The Indians had the skill to trap these animals, and they traded the pelts for firearms, or metal tools, glass beads, and other English trinkets. Such knickknacks were often poorly made and of little value.

As more English crowded into the colonies, most of the wildlife moved westward into the unsettled wilderness. The Indians had to follow the beavers, foxes, and other animals if they were to trade the same number of pelts. All too often, this meant moving onto land belonging to

Early colonists traded with Native Americans and often cheated them

When European settlers came to the New World, they brought with them many contagious diseases such as smallpox, measles, typhoid, cholera, and syphilis. These diseases were new to the Indians, so their bodies had developed no way to resist them. An epidemic could wipe out an entire Indian nation in a matter of weeks. It is estimated that 25 to 50 percent of the North American Indian population of nearly 5 million died from European diseases between 1800 and 1900.

neighboring tribes. As a result, almost constant warfare broke out among the Indians.

The colonists also pressured the Indians to sell their land. Many colonists cheated the Indians. They would pay only a small portion of the price they had promised to pay, or they simply settled on land outside of the purchased territory.

The colonists tainted Indian culture in many ways. They gave the Indians large quantities of alcohol, and soon alcoholism became a serious problem for many tribes. Schools built to "civilize" the Indians tried to make them live like Europeans. And Christian missionaries worked tirelessly to wipe out native religions.

The Indians grew tired of being cheated and forced off their land. They fought back. For example, in the 1670s, the New England colonies barely survived an attack by an Indian Confederation. And in the 1760s, colonists moving west onto the frontier were driven back about 100 miles by a great alliance of Ohio Valley tribes.

However, Indian bravery was no match

Native Americans helped colonist Roger Williams establish Rhode Island

for English guns. The colonists' attacks on the Indians became increasingly brutal, and powerful Indian chiefs were murdered one by one. Eventually, most Indian tribes were forced to live on reservations. They lost their freedom and many of their traditional ways.

Hundreds of thousands of Native Americans died from European diseases

23

FOUR EARLY ENGLISH AMERICANS

Anne Hutchinson (1591–1643)

The daughter of a well-known English preacher, young Anne grew up surrounded by the buzz of religious and philosophical discussions. She married William Hutchinson in 1612 and had 14 children.

In 1633, her eldest son immigrated to the Massachusetts Bay Colony with John Cotton, a preacher whom Anne Hutchinson greatly admired. The following year, she and her family immigrated as well.

In Massachusetts Bay, Hutchinson was respected for her intelligence. She was a self-taught expert on the Bible, and her curious mind led her to become very involved in religion.

The trial of Anne Hutchinson

Hutchinson organized large meetings of women in her Boston home. There they would discuss the sermons of the previous Sunday. At these meetings, Hutchinson talked about her own religious beliefs, which disagreed with Puritan teachings. She wanted to do away with church laws. She believed religion should be a private affair between an individual and God.

As a result, in 1637 Hutchinson was put on trial for "traducing (slandering) the ministers" of Massachusetts Bay, and she was banished from the colony. Along with her family, she then helped establish the colony of Rhode Island. In 1642, she moved to what is now Long Island, New York, where she was killed by Indians.

Benjamin Franklin (1706–1790)

Benjamin Franklin was probably the most famous American of the 1700s. During his long career as a politician, Franklin was a key figure in preparing the American colonies for their war of independence from Great Britain. He persuaded the French to help the colonies with supplies of money and weapons. And he helped create the U.S. Constitution, which has remained the backbone of American government for over 200 years.

What made Franklin so unique, however, were his accomplishments outside of politics. Franklin invented bifocal eyeglasses, the lightning rod, and a stove that kept a room warmer than a fireplace. He helped found a library, a hospital, and a firefighting team. He started a school that eventually grew into the University of

Benjamin Franklin experimenting with electricity

Pennsylvania. He designed scientific experiments to learn more about the nature of electricity, and his results were hailed all over Europe as well as in America.

Franklin was intelligent, witty, and broad-minded. He did not wear a powdered wig, as did many men in his day, or think he was better than anyone else. He dressed in plain brown clothes and believed that everyone, whether rich or poor, deserved an education. Franklin's ideas were very popular in France and helped to inspire the French Revolution, which began in 1789.

Sarah Grimké (1792–1873)
Angelina Grimké (1805–1879)

Sarah and Angelina were born into a wealthy slave-holding family in South Carolina. At an early age, the sisters believed that slavery was wrong. Sarah wanted to study law to help fight slavery, but women were not allowed to attend law school at that time.

In 1835, Angelina wrote a letter to William Garrison, the leader of the abolition (anti-slavery) movement, praising him for his work. To her surprise, Garrison published the letter. This encouraged Angelina to become more active in the abolition movement. She began writing thoughtful articles urging southern women to speak and act against slavery.

Angelina and Sarah became very convincing speakers. At first, they spoke only to small groups of women. But soon, they gave lectures in front of large audiences of women and men. In those days, public speaking by women was considered shocking, and the Grimké sisters were harshly criticized. So they became defenders of women's rights as well as champions of the abolition movement.

Sarah Grimké

Angelina Grimké

THE AMERICAN REVOLUTION

For more than 100 years, England and France battled each other to gain control of territory and trade in North America. The competition between them finally exploded in the Seven Years' War, which lasted from 1756 to 1763. England won the war, along with great stretches of land west of the colonies.

The war with France had been expensive. England wanted the colonists to help pay for the costs through additional taxes. The colonists were already paying taxes on goods shipped to and from the colonies. They thought this was enough. But England went ahead and passed new laws like the Stamp Act, which taxed all printed materials, such as newspapers and legal documents.

Throughout English history, kings and queens had tried to collect unfair taxes from the English people. English citizens fought long and hard to make sure they would be taxed only with the approval of their representatives—people elected to look out for their interests. As a result, the English people, and also the English in America, were very sensitive about the subject of taxes.

The new taxes like the Stamp Act were *direct* taxes. Direct taxes went straight to England, where Parliament decided how

Thomas Jefferson, third president of the United States

The Bettmann Archive

As a young man, Thomas Jefferson wrote essays against England and became known as a fine writer. Later in life, he drew on the ideas of John Locke and wrote the Declaration of Independence almost entirely by himself. It was approved and signed by delegates from all the colonies on July 4, 1776. In 1803, Jefferson became the third president of the United States. He served two terms. Afterwards, he worked to design and build the University of Virginia. Jefferson died on July 4, 1826, the 50th anniversary of the signing of the Declaration of Independence.

the money should be spent. But there were no representatives from the colonies in British Parliament. That meant the colonists had no say in how *their* money would be spent.

Each of the colonies sent representatives, called delegates, to town meetings to protest the taxes. Riots broke out in many towns, and angry mobs threatened tax collectors. Many colonists refused to pay the stamp taxes, even though English officials punished them with fines and imprisonment.

The final break between England and the 13 colonies had begun. English American patriots, such as James Otis and Samuel Adams, rallied for war. Otis argued that the new taxes violated the rights of the colonists. Adams gave passionate speeches that made many colonists eager to fight against England and win their independence.

General George Washington with his troops at Valley Forge

When war finally broke out in April 1775, it was not supported by all of the colonists. Many felt closer ties to England than they did towards each other. But there was a quite a difference between the English in the colonies and the English back home.

Some colonists had been in America for four generations—that's more than 100 years. They no longer knew their relatives back in England. The colonists copied English customs, dress, and form of government, but they changed them just enough to give them an "American" feel. The close-knit Puritan communities in New England were an American creation. So were the ethnically diverse cities of Pennsylvania and the large plantations in the South. Even the English language changed in accent and usage, since people from many different regions of England and Europe spoke it in their own way in the colonies.

When the English colonists won the Revolutionary War, they had already become a new and distinct group of people. They had become English Americans.

The famous Boston Tea Party was a protest against taxes

27

PART III: THE POST-COLONIAL PERIOD TO THE PRESENT

THE INDUSTRIAL REVOLUTION

After the Revolutionary War ended in 1783, few English immigrants came to America. Many English citizens believed it would be disloyal to do so because America was no longer a part of the British Empire. Gradually, relations between England and America became friendlier, and small numbers of English men and women sailed for the United States.

Between 1815 and 1860, more than 600,000 English immigrants arrived in American ports. Some of these newcomers were unemployed farmers looking for work. But most had left their homeland because of widespread social changes caused by the Industrial Revolution.

During the Industrial Revolution, great advances were made in technology. The steam engine provided power to run machinery, and the power loom made it possible to produce large amounts of cloth. Factories manufactured everything from clothes to tin cans.

Cities grew quickly during the Industrial Revolution. This is Norfolk, Virginia, around 1900.

The inventions of two English Americans greatly influenced the Industrial Revolution in the U.S. These were Eli Whitney's cotton gin and Isaac Singer's sewing machine. Eli Whitney invented the cotton gin in the 1790s. Before cotton could be sold, tiny seeds had to be removed from the raw product. Seed-picking by hand took a long time. The cotton gin increased the amount of cotton that could be seeded in one day by 300 percent! As a result, cotton became a profitable crop, and the demand for slaves increased in the South. Isaac Singer invented the sewing machine in 1840. The sewing machine made it possible to produce large quantities of clothing quickly and cheaply. Finally, store-bought clothes were not just a luxury for the rich, but a convenience everyone could afford.

The new technology completely changed English society. For hundreds of years, English goods had been handmade by skilled craftsmen. After the Industrial Revolution began, machines made the same goods faster and cheaper. The skills of metal-workers, carpenters, seamstresses, and other artisans were suddenly useless. Millions of people were put out of work.

Men and women streamed into overcrowded cities hoping to find work in factories. This created fierce competition for jobs. As a result, English laborers were overworked and underpaid. They could not afford proper housing and had to live in run-down slums. City streets swarmed with pickpockets, and crime became common.

Many English people began to look to America as a possible escape from their

The power loom made it possible to produce great quantities of fabric

soot-filled cities and dreary lives. But for most, the transportation fares were too expensive. However, between 1815 and 1820 England tripled the number of ships sailing to and from America.

On voyages from America to England, the ships carried full loads of lumber, cotton, or tobacco. On voyages from England to America, however, the ships were not full and had room to transport people. As a result, ship fares dropped from $60 in 1815 to $15 in 1820. Now, even poor families could afford to set sail for America.

In America, the Industrial Revolution created many jobs. Huge factories popped up in northern cities. A great number of workers were needed to operate the machines, so most English immigrants had no problem finding jobs. They still worked long hours, and their lives were not easy. But in America, English immigrants had more opportunities to improve their lives.

Isaac Singer invented the sewing machine in 1840. Here, a worker makes shoes.

THE WAVE OF IMMIGRATION

During the American Civil War (1861–1865), immigration to America came to a halt. Few English people cared to start a new life in a war-torn country. But afterwards, between 1865 and 1914, some 3 million English immigrants swarmed onto America's shores.

This huge wave of immigration was caused in part by a population explosion back in England. There were too many people and not enough jobs. Also, by the 1860s, steamships rather than sailing vessels began carrying passengers to America.

On the sailing vessels, the journey to America had lasted about two months. The passengers suffered from constant seasickness, poor food, and cramped quarters, and many caught deadly diseases. The faster steamships shortened the journey to only 15 days, saving the travelers from

Immigrants had to pass a health exam before they were allowed into the country

Newcomers leaving Ellis Island, the main immigrant station

During World War I (1914–1918), many jobs were created in England and all English ships were used to fight the war. Because of this, almost no English citizens immigrated during this time. After the war, America passed many laws that restricted immigration, and only about 35,000 English immigrants came to America each year. Instead, many English men and women left for English colonies in Africa, Asia, Australia, or Canada.

many of these horrors. The speedy trips also made it possible to carry more English immigrants to America.

But it was opportunity that drew most English immigrants to the United States. In America, cities were still growing, and factories were built throughout the Northeast. Jobs were plentiful. Immigrants easily found work in the factories and mills along the eastern coast, coal mines in Pennsylvania, and the new steel companies in Indiana and Ohio.

In addition, the West was opening up from the Mississippi River to the California coast. Land was cheap, and the U.S. government promoted settlement by forcing Native Americans off their land. English farmers were lured to America with dreams of owning their own farms. They bought land on the western prairies and built their farms from scratch.

Many English immigrants learned about opportunities in America from advertisements. Factories needed thousands of workers to operate the machines, and railroad companies needed farmers to settle land near train stations out west. American businessmen sent agents to England to convince people to immigrate. The agents told unhappy farmers and factory workers how they could travel to America cheaply, find decent, well-paying jobs, and buy land at reasonable prices. They persuaded many people to come to America.

Until the late 1800s, America was still mainly an "English" country. The American government, language, and culture had come chiefly from the English. However, during the late 1800s millions of people immigrated not only from England, but also from Germany, Italy, Ireland, Poland, and other countries. When the English immigrants sailed into New York's Ellis Island, the port bustled with people from all over the world.

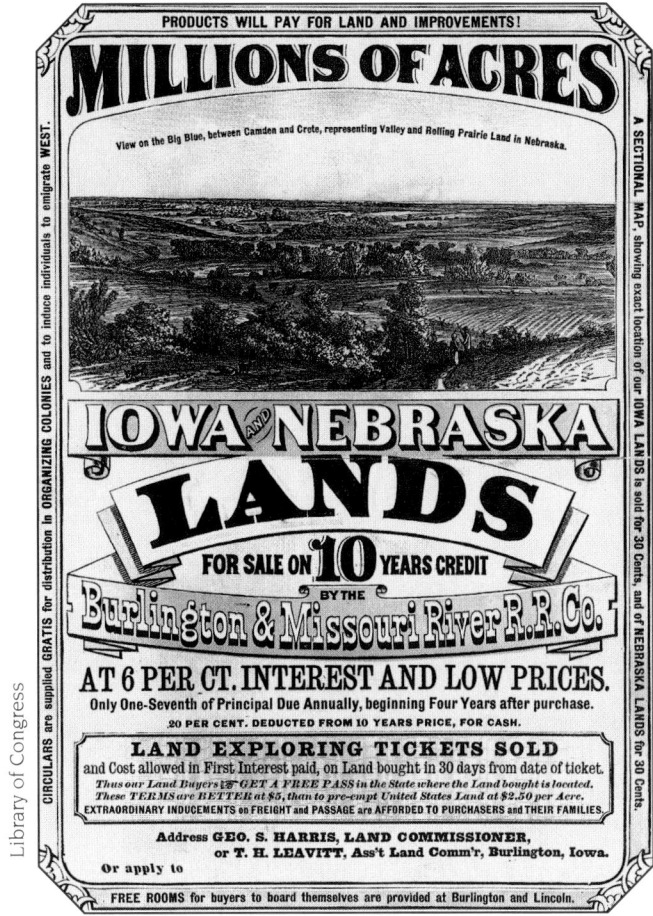

Advertisements for farmland in the West lured immigrants to America

These ethnic groups changed the personality of our country with their unique culture and customs. Some English Americans, especially those whose families had lived here for generations, looked down on the changes. They saw the new immigrants and their cultures as "un-American." They also blamed non-English immigrants for creating competition for jobs, which caused wages to fall. Although English Americans made many contributions to our country, they also began a trend to discriminate against immigrants from other nations.

LIFE AND WORK IN THE NEW COUNTRY

Life in America could be quite confusing for new immigrants. After leaving their ships, they had to start their lives all over again. The first step was to find a low-priced room to rent. The next step was to find a job, and then a family home.

English immigrants usually settled in the northeastern states, especially Pennsylvania and New Jersey. Very few of them went south, especially before the Civil War, because most of the work there was done by unpaid slaves. Nobody wanted to pay wages for English men and women.

English immigrants who did not have special skills were offered the roughest, dirtiest jobs. They became manual laborers and swung their picks and shovels throughout the city streets. Paid very low wages, these workers could afford only to live in dirty slums. In addition, the hard labor in the hot summers and freezing winters caused many to become ill.

The majority of English immigrants found jobs in factories and mills. They worked hard—usually 11 hours a day, 6 days a week. But they were paid three to four times more than they had made in England. They could afford to live in decent houses, eat well-balanced meals, and buy an occasional treat, like a sofa or new shoes.

Many English factory and mill owners closed their factories in England and built new ones in America, where they hoped to make a bigger profit. But these owners did not want to have to train a whole new staff.

Even children worked in factories such as this Massachusetts textile mill

Many immigrants were persuaded to come to America by wild tales that described the country as a paradise with streets paved with gold. These people were often very disappointed when they arrived. This was especially true in the late 1800s. During that period, millions of immigrants came to America from all over Europe. The number of unemployed people was greater than the number of jobs available, so many could not find work. Unable to find the American Dream, thousands of English men and women returned to England.

32

Many immigrants found industrial jobs

Instead, they often paid for their old workers to move to America to work in the new factories and mills.

For example, so many textile workers from Bradford, England, moved to Lawrence, Massachusetts, that the town was nicknamed the "Bradford of America." A section of another Massachusetts town, Lowell, was known as "English Row" because so many English immigrants lived there.

In the late 1800s, about 15,000 silk workers moved from England's silk mills to new mills opening in Paterson, New Jersey. In 1883, lace makers from Nottingham left England to work in Brooklyn, New York. And a large number of knife makers from Sheffield, England, moved to Waterbury, Connecticut. An English mill worker might find herself doing the same job in a factory with her same childhood friends, only in a different country!

However, most English immigrants did not live side by side with other English immigrants. They lived in many different towns and cities throughout the country, where they found work as iron or steel workers, coal miners, printers, managers, and farmers. They were rarely discriminated against because they blended into American society. With few opportunities closed to them, English immigrants quickly and quietly became English Americans.

English American children helped out on family farms

WESTWARD HO!

Most English immigrants settled in the eastern cities. But some 2 million others braved the wild woodlands and prairies of the West. Along with immigrants from other countries, especially Germany, Norway, and Sweden, they became pioneer farmers. Between 1840 and 1900, the pioneers settled almost all of the land from the Mississippi River to the Pacific Ocean.

The native peoples who had lived in these regions for hundreds of years saw their land taken away by the white settlers. Many Native Americans were killed by settlers or the U.S. Army. Most of those who survived were forced onto reservations.

The two main routes leading west were the Oregon Trail and the Santa Fe Trail. Both trails began in Independence, Missouri. In the early days, pioneers gathered in Independence from all over the country.

The English Kitchen served meals for 20 cents in Round Pond, Oklahoma, in the 1890s

The pioneers grouped their canvas-covered wagons, called Conestogas, into "wagon trains." Wagon trains made the westward journey safer. Indians defending their territory and dangerous outlaws were less likely to attack a large number of armed people traveling together. Also, if a family's wagon broke down, there were other people around to help repair it.

Most schools in the West, such as this sod schoolhouse in Oklahoma in 1895, were one-room buildings

Pioneer children were encouraged to go to school. But most children had to tend the farm animals, milk the cows, find fuel, and fetch water. They did not have much time to study. Besides, good teachers were hard to find. In a small California town, all one man had to do to become a teacher was spell *cat, hat, rat,* and *mat*!

Most English immigrants ventured out west in the late 1800s. By then, trains ran from the Ohio Valley all the way to the Pacific Coast. The new railroad made the pioneers' journey much easier. They could ride the railroad deep into the western plains and then set off in their wagons. This shortened the trip from a few months to just a few weeks.

Pioneer life was difficult. In wooded areas, the settlers faced the task of cutting down hundreds of trees. This created a cleared area for planting crops. The trees were chopped into logs and used to build the family home.

Many families settled on the Great Plains, a vast area sweeping from the Missouri River west to the Rocky Mountains and from Texas north into Canada. On the plains, the land was hard, dry, and difficult to plow. People used heavy bricks of prairie earth, called sod, to build their houses. Sod houses were crude, but they stayed warm in the winter and cool in the summer.

Thousands of pioneers moved out west to take advantage of the Homestead Act of 1862. This Act offered 160 acres of land to anyone who wanted it, for just $18. All a family had to do was farm the land for five years.

Pioneer children often tended the farm animals. These youngsters are taking a break from their chores.

Once an area became settled, a town was built. Most western towns had a church, general store, blacksmith, hotel, sheriff's office, and saloon. Some saloons were wild, lawless places where outlaws and tough pioneers engaged in brawls and gunfights. But most were peaceful places where farmers gathered for a good laugh and a drink with friends.

On weekends and holidays, pioneer families socialized at church, square dances, and picnics where they feasted on barbecued buffalo meat. They were entertained by magicians, snake charmers, sword swallowers, and circuses that traveled throughout the West. The plays of William Shakespeare were also very popular. Many theatergoers recited the lines right along with the actors.

More than 2 million English immigrants headed west to become farmers

MAKING PROGRESS IN AMERICA

To many immigrants, the American Dream simply meant earning good wages, owning one's own home, and having enough spare time to relax and enjoy life. Out of all the immigrant groups searching for the American Dream, the English, on the whole, had the easiest time finding it.

Other immigrant groups, especially those from eastern and southern Europe, achieved success more slowly. It often took two generations before many of these immigrants could afford to move out of the city slums. Only after three or four generations did large numbers of them go to college or enter professional careers.

English immigrants were able to improve their lot in life much more quickly

A stylish couple pose with their bicycle-built-for-two in Washington, D.C., around 1885

First Lady Hillary Rodham Clinton

Just three generations after her family came to the United States from England, First Lady Hillary Rodham Clinton has become one of the most powerful women in the country. Hillary's great-grandfather, a coal miner, came to the U.S. in 1881. His son worked in a lace factory. His son, Hillary's father, finished college and became a successful businessman. Hillary herself is a Yale Law School graduate and a highly respected lawyer. She has worked tirelessly to protect the rights of children and to help make health care available to all Americans.

because they had no language barriers and suffered the least from prejudice. For example, it was not unusual for the sons and daughters of factory workers and farmers to move into professional careers after just one generation.

In addition, English Americans did not live in "English" neighborhoods or stay in just one part of the country. They were comfortable enough in America to move where they would be offered the best opportunities. As a result, English Americans skipped many of the hardships other ethnic groups had to face.

English Americans founded the government of our nation. And they continued to make contributions in politics throughout our history. One measure of their success is the large number of English Americans who have become presidents. Over one-half of our nation's presidents were either wholly or partly English in heritage.

English Americans also have written most of the famous novels and short stories in American literature. Among the long list of English American writers are Edgar Allan Poe and William Faulkner. Poe wrote creepy stories of mystery and terror. Faulkner, a southern novelist, received the

The New England general store was a gathering place for neighbors and friends

Nobel Prize for literature in 1949. The Nobel Prize is one of the most important awards for writing in the world.

One of this country's best loved poets was the English American Robert Frost (1874–1963). Frost was awarded a gold medal by the United States Congress for his excellent poetry.

In the 1950s, the United States changed its immigration laws and began to favor immigrants with special skills. Over 400,000 English immigrants have come to this country since that time. Most of these immigrants have been well-educated professionals such as doctors, nurses, computer experts, businesspeople, and teachers.

On the whole, these new English immigrants have achieved success in their new home. Like the English immigrants who came to America before them, these newcomers have moved easily into the mainstream of American life.

After a few generations, many English Americans achieved the American Dream

FAMOUS ENGLISH AMERICANS

Clara Barton, founder of the Red Cross

Clara Barton (1821–1912)
Clara Barton, known as the "angel of the battlefield," was one of America's most famous fighters for human rights. During the Civil War, Barton set up an agency that gave medical supplies to help wounded soldiers. Afterwards, she founded an organization to search for missing soldiers. Barton also worked to make sure prisoners of war were treated with compassion.

In 1881, Clara Barton achieved her greatest triumph by founding the American Red Cross. The Red Cross organizes relief efforts during war and natural disasters such as earthquakes. The Red Cross also helps save lives by encouraging people to donate blood.

Emily Dickinson (1830–1886)
Emily Dickinson was one of America's greatest poets. Her poems are usually about love, death, or nature. They are generally short and powerful, with rhythmic lines that seem to hit the reader like a series of harsh pokes.

Dickinson lived a very withdrawn and private life. She never married, rarely traveled, and preferred to keep in touch with her friends by writing letters. In fact, for the last 20 years of her life, she never left the boundaries of her family's property! She dressed all in white and received few visitors.

Although Dickinson wrote some 1,775 poems, she only allowed seven to be published during her lifetime. Luckily, after Emily died her sister had many of her poems published. Because of her lonely, mysterious life and the subject matter of her poems, Dickinson has often been called "the New England mystic."

Emily Dickinson, American poet

Author Mark Twain

Mark Twain (1835–1910)

Samuel Langhorne Clemens, better known as Mark Twain, spent his childhood in Hannibal, Missouri, alongside the Mississippi River. He spent his days fishing, playing pirate or Robin Hood on a nearby island, or simply watching the river. He also met all sorts of unusual characters—professional gamblers, wandering drunks, and tough, quick-fisted outlaws.

Twain's boyhood memories gave him the material for many of his books, especially *The Adventures of Tom Sawyer* and *The Adventures of Huckleberry Finn*. Simply written in the language of ordinary people, both of these novels were smash hits.

Besides being one of America's greatest novelists, Twain was a popular lecturer both at home and in Europe. He fascinated audiences with exciting stories and tall tales. He also talked about more serious issues, like slavery, with honesty and concern. The wit and wisdom in Twain's work made him a national celebrity.

Wilbur Wright (1867–1912)
Orville Wright (1871–1948)

Wilbur and Orville Wright were mechanical geniuses. They built bicycles and machines that printed newspapers and books. Using their many talents, they set out to build a flying machine—the world's first airplane.

The Wright brothers used nature as their guide. Wilbur and Orville watched the way buzzards keep their balance in the air. They noticed that the birds control their flight by tilting their wings up and down or left and right. The Wright brothers made sure that their airplane also had wings that could be tilted.

The brothers' first flying machine, called the *Kitty Hawk*, was finished in 1903. The *Kitty Hawk*'s first flight lasted only 12 seconds. But just five years later, the Wright brothers built a machine that stayed in the air for a whopping 2 hours and 20 minutes!

Wilbur died of typhoid in 1912. But Orville continued to make valuable contributions in aviation—the science of flying airplanes—until his death in 1948.

Orville and Wilbur Wright testing their first flying machine

THOMAS EDISON

Perhaps one afternoon you watched a movie, listened to some records, and played with one of your talking dolls. That night, you flipped on a light switch and read before falling asleep. Motion pictures, record players, electric lights, and even talking dolls are only a few of the many inventions created by Thomas Alva Edison (1847–1931).

Thomas Edison was nine years old when he first became interested in science. His parents had given him a book called *Parker's Natural and Experimental Philosophy*, which he read eagerly. Afterwards, he decided to become a scientist, and he set up a laboratory in his basement. Strange odors, smoke, and small explosions often came from this mysterious laboratory.

When Edison turned 12, he worked full-time on a train as a "candy butcher." His job was to sell newspapers, sandwiches, and snacks to the passengers. In the back of the train, he built a small laboratory. Whenever he was not busy, he performed experiments, tinkered with motors, or just figured out how different machines worked.

Edison listening to an early phonograph, one of his inventions

People were amazed by electric light, invented in 1879

Thomas Edison created his incandescent lamp by passing a current of electricity through a very fine wire inside a glass globe. The resulting "light bulb" gave off much more light than fire and worked in an entirely new way. Imagine how amazed people were to see light created for the first time without the use of fire. Crowds flocked to Menlo Park just as they would to a fair to admire the electric lights on the streets near Edison's famous laboratory.

Thomas Edison with the first motion picture machine

Edison became a telegraph operator when he was 16. The telegraph let people send messages to others far away by tapping out a code of dots and dashes (called Morse Code) across a wire. At first, each telegraph wire could send or receive only one message at a time. Edison created a device called a quadruplex that could send or receive up to four messages at a time.

In 1869, Edison received $40,000 for one of his inventions—a huge amount of money at that time. As a result, he could finally afford to become a full-time inventor. He built himself a laboratory in Menlo Park, New Jersey, in 1876. By then he had received over 100 patents, which are records that give inventors full credit for their creations. These patents were for new inventions or improvements of existing machines.

At Menlo Park, Edison found a way to improve the sound quality of the telephone, which had been recently invented by Alexander Graham Bell. Edison's experiments with the telephone led him to work on a "talking machine." This machine developed into the phonograph. Invented in 1877, it was the world's first record player.

Thomas Edison's most popular invention, in 1879, was the "incandescent lamp," or electric light bulb. Before this invention, homes and city streets were lit by candles or gaslights. These light sources were troublesome and unsafe. Smoke from burning gas damaged the interiors of homes and fire was a constant threat.

During Thomas Edison's lifetime, he was issued 1,093 patents, more than any other inventor in history. Americans nicknamed him the "Wizard of Menlo Park." However, it was not "wizardry" but long hours of work that made him so successful. "Genius," Thomas Edison once said, "is 1 percent inspiration and 99 percent perspiration."

THE ENGLISH AMERICAN

The English continue to come to America today, although in much smaller numbers. Immigration first began to slow after World War I. At that time, the United States passed laws that made it difficult for immigrants to come to this country. During World War II, nearly a million English soldiers were killed. And young men, as many of these soldiers were, had been the most likely to immigrate.

After 1950, a different type of English immigrant began to come to America. The United States changed its laws so that most immigrants allowed into the country had to have special skills. Since then, over 400,000 English men and women have immigrated to this country. Most of them have been doctors, nurses, engineers, computer programmers, teachers, and other professionals. They settled all over the country but especially in New York, Massachusetts, and California.

Today, English Americans are the third-largest ethnic group in the United States. (German Americans and Irish Americans are first and second.) The most recent numbers show that a fifth of all Americans

A World War II soldier welcomes his "war bride" to America

During World War II (1939–1945), about 2 million American soldiers were sent to England. Many of these soldiers were young, single men. In their free time, they began meeting English women at pubs, dances, and social events. Many of these meetings blossomed into romances and marriage proposals. About 100,000 English women, half of whom served in the British Armed Forces, married American servicemen. These women were called "war brides." There was a lot of excitement about the arrival of the war brides in America. Many people thought that the marriages showed how close America and England had become from working together during the war.

consider themselves at least partly English by heritage. Although the English are not the largest ethnic group, they have influenced America more than any other group.

The English have shaped this country in countless ways. Our language, form of government, dress, building styles, literature, and common social practices are all chiefly English creations. Baseball, considered to be "as American as apple pie," evolved from an English children's game called rounders. English folk songs, sung first by colonists and later by immigrants who settled the West, became a part of American folk music as well.

Even though the English have contributed so much to this country, they often are overlooked as an ethnic group. In fact, English Americans have been nicknamed "the invisible immigrants." How could the English be called invisible? One answer is that English immigrants had so much in common with Americans, they blended into this country without notice.

For example, imagine you go to a school in another country where most of the kids look different, act different, and speak a different language. Then imagine you discover there are other Americans in the class. Chances are you would, at least at first, band together with the Americans. This is

English Americans founded many of the nation's top colleges and universities

because, familiar with their language and habits, it would be easier to make friends.

Now imagine going to a school in another country where the kids act, dress, and speak the *same* language as you. Chances are, if there were other Americans in the class, you would not band together in a separate group. Instead, you would blend in, because you had many things in common with the rest of the class.

Likewise, immigrants from Italy, Poland, China, and other countries usually did not speak English and were not familiar with American ways. These ethnic groups commonly formed their own separate neighborhoods so they could feel at home. They were seen by others as a unique group with their own language, food, and way of life.

English immigrants, however, had many things in common with Americans. For the most part, there was no such thing as an "English" neighborhood. The English did not feel a need to stick together. Instead, they found work in all parts of the country, and so did not stand out as a distinct ethnic group.

A family enjoys a game of croquet, a favorite English pastime

43

The main contributions the English made to America are in government, language, religion, and education

In addition, many Americans noticed, and sometimes disliked, other ethnic groups for their differences—because they were shorter, or darker, or believed in a different religion. Compared with most Americans, English immigrants did not stand out as different. They could not be identified as a group by any special feature.

Even though the English blended in to American society, there are still some things in America that are considered typically English. Pubs and saloons with dart boards, restaurants serving English food (like kidney pies and Yorkshire pudding), and rugby teams are all clearly English in origin. But the really significant English contributions to this country—such as our language, form of government, and major religion (Protestantism)—are rarely thought of as English. They are so much a part of our everyday lives that their origins are hard to see.

Over time, most English beliefs and customs have changed just enough so that they are now thought of as "American." So it is important that we remember just how much the English Americans have contributed to our country, from the early colonists to the Revolutionary War and up to the present day.

INDEX

Adams, Samuel, 27
American Red Cross, 38
Barton, Clara, 38
Bill of Rights, 5
Black Death, 7
Boleyn, Anne, 10
Boston Tea Party, 26
Calvert, Cecil, 18
Catherine of Aragon, 10
Catholic Church, 10-11
Catholics
    in America, 18, 20
    in England, 10
Charles I (king of England), 5, 13
Charles II (king of England), 17, 18
Children
    during the Middle Ages, 6
    in the North, 20-21
    pioneer children, 34-35
    schooling of, 21
    in the South, 21
Church of England, 10-11
Clinton, Hillary Rodham, 36
Colonists, English
    in colonial times, 2, 14-21
    convicts, 12
    crossing the Atlantic, 13
    first settlers, 14-15
    life in the colonies, 20-21
    reasons for emigrating, 2-3, 13
    in the American Revolution, 26-27
Colonization of America, 12-13
Columbus, Christopher, 12, 22
Connecticut, 17
Cotton, 18-19, 28
Cotton gin, 28
Cromwell, Oliver, 5
Dickinson, Emily, 38
Edison, Thomas, 40-41
Elizabeth I (queen of England), 11
Ellis Island, 30-31
England
    early history of, 4-5
    in the Middle Ages, 6-7
    religion in, 7, 10-11
    religious intolerance in, 10-11, 12-13
    in the 17th century, 8-9
    unemployment in, 13
Farmers
    in America, 31, 34-35
    in England, 8-9
Faulkner, William, 37
Fawkes, Guy, 10
Feudalism 4, 6-7
Franklin, Benjamin, 20, 24-25
Frost, Robert, 37
Georgia, 18
Gilbert, Sir Humphrey, 12
Grimké, Angelina and Sarah, 25
Harold II (king of England), 4
Henry VIII (king of England), 10-11
Homestead Act of 1862, 35
Hooker, Reverend Thomas, 16-17
Hutchinson, Anne, 24
Immigrants, English
    arrival after 1950, 37, 42
    crossing the Atlantic, 29, 30-31
    employment of, 32-33
    pioneers, 34-35
    prejudice among, 31
    reasons for emigrating, 28-29, 30-31
    social advances of, 33, 36-37
    war brides, 42
Indentured servants, 19, 21
Industrial Revolution, 18, 28-29
James I (king of England), 11, 13
Jamestown Colony, 14-15
Jefferson, Thomas, 4, 26
John (king of England), 4-5
Locke, John, 4

Magna Carta, 5
Maryland, 18
Massachusetts Bay Colony, 16
Mayflower, 14-15
Mayflower Compact, 14
Middle Ages, 6-7
Native Americans
    effects of European diseases on, 22
    enslavement of, 22
    trade with colonists, 22
    unfair treatment of, 22-23, 31
New York City, 17
North Carolina, 18
Otis, James, 27
Parliament, 5, 10
Penn, William, 17
Pennsylvania, 17
Pilgrims, 14-15
Pioneers, 34-35
Plymouth Colony, 14-15
Pocahontas, 15
Poe, Edgar Allan, 37
Powhatan, 15
Puritans, 11, 13, 14-15, 16, 20-21
Quakers (Society of Friends), 17, 20
Raleigh, Sir Walter, 12
Religion
    in America, 16-17, 20
    in England, 10-11
    intolerance in, 16-17
Revolutionary War, 3, 26-27

Rhode Island, 17
Rolfe, John, 15
Salem Witch Trials, 16
Separatists, 11, 15
Sewing machine, 28
Shakespeare, William, 8, 35
Singer, Isaac, 28
Slavery, 18-19, 28, 32
    advantages of in the North, 19
    on southern plantations, 18-19
    treatment of slaves, 19
South Carolina, 18
Spanish Armada, 12
Squanto, 15
Stamp Act, 26
Stowe, Harriet Beecher, 18
Thanksgiving, 15
Tobacco, 15, 18
Tull, Jethro, 9
Twain, Mark, 39
Webster, Noah, 20
Westward expansion, 31, 34-35
Whitney, Eli, 28
William the Conqueror, 4
William and Mary (king and queen of England), 13
Williams, Reverend Roger, 16-17
Winthrop, John, 16
World War I, 30
World War II, 42
Wright, Orville and Wilbur, 39

Other books about English Americans:

Blumenthal, Shirley and Jerome S. Ozer. *Coming to America: Immigrants from the British Isles.* New York: Delacorte, 1980.

Cates, Edwin H. *The English in America.* Minneapolis: Lerner Publications Co., 1966.

Colonial America. Grand Rapids: Gateway Press, Inc., 1988.

Cornelius, James M. *The English Americans.* New York: Chelsea House Publishers, 1990.

Ferguson, Sheila. *Village and Town Life.* London: Batsford Academic and Educational Ltd., 1983.

More Great Books for Kids Ages 8 and Up
For a Free Catalog Call 1-800-888-7504

EXTREMELY WEIRD SERIES

All of the titles are written by Sarah Lovett, 8½" x 11", 48 pages, $9.95 paperback, $14.95 hardcover, with color photographs and illustrations.

Extremely Weird Bats
Extremely Weird Birds
Extremely Weird Endangered Species
Extremely Weird Fishes
Extremely Weird Frogs
Extremely Weird Insects
Extremely Weird Mammals
Extremely Weird Micro Monsters
Extremely Weird Primates
Extremely Weird Reptiles
Extremely Weird Sea Creatures
Extremely Weird Snakes
Extremely Weird Spiders

X-RAY VISION SERIES

Each title in the series is 8½" x 11", 48 pages, $9.95 paperback, with color photographs and illustrations, and written by Ron Schultz.

Looking Inside the Brain
Looking Inside Cartoon Animation
Looking Inside Caves and Caverns
Looking Inside Sports Aerodynamics
Looking Inside Sunken Treasure
Looking Inside Telescopes and the Night Sky

THE KIDDING AROUND TRAVEL GUIDES

All of the titles listed below are 64 pages and $9.95 paperbacks, except for *Kidding Around the National Parks* and *Kidding Around Spain*, which are 108 pages and $12.95 paperbacks.

Kidding Around Atlanta
Kidding Around Boston, 2nd ed.
Kidding Around Chicago, 2nd ed.
Kidding Around the Hawaiian Islands
Kidding Around London
Kidding Around Los Angeles
Kidding Around the National Parks
    of the Southwest
Kidding Around New York City, 2nd ed.
Kidding Around Paris
Kidding Around Philadelphia
Kidding Around San Diego
Kidding Around San Francisco
Kidding Around Santa Fe
Kidding Around Seattle
Kidding Around Spain
Kidding Around Washington, D.C., 2nd ed.

MASTERS OF MOTION SERIES

Each title in the series is 10¼" x 9", 48 pages, $9.95 paperback, with color photographs and illustrations.

How to Drive an Indy Race Car
   David Rubel
How to Fly a 747
   Tim Paulson
How to Fly the Space Shuttle
   Russell Shorto

THE KIDS EXPLORE SERIES

Each title is written by kids for kids by the Westridge Young Writers Workshop, 7" x 9", and $9.95 paperback, with photographs and illustrations by the kids.

Kids Explore America's Hispanic Heritage
112 pages
Kids Explore America's African American Heritage 128 pages
Kids Explore the Gifts of Children with Special Needs 128 pages
Kids Explore America's Japanese American Heritage 144 pages

ENVIRONMENTAL TITLES

Habitats: *Where the Wild Things Live*
Randi Hacker and Jackie Kaufman
8½" x 11", 48 pages, color illustrations, $9.95 paper

The Indian Way: *Learning to Communicate with Mother Earth*
Gary McLain
7" x 9", 114 pages, two-color illustrations, $9.95 paper

Rads, Ergs, and Cheeseburgers: *The Kids' Guide to Energy and the Environment*
Bill Yanda
7" x 9", 108 pages, two-color illustrations, $13.95 paper

The Kids' Environment Book: *What's Awry and Why*
Anne Pedersen
7" x 9", 192 pages, two-color illustrations, $13.95 paper

DATE DUE